THE JOURNEY HOME

AN AMERICAN FAMILY™ BOOK FOUR: 1827

The Journey Home

LUCY JANE BLEDSOE

FEARON/JANUS/QUERCUS
Belmont, California

Simon & Schuster Supplementary Education Group

AN AMERICAN FAMILY™ SERIES

Book One: Colony of Fear
Book Two: A Matter of Pride
Book Three: Two Kinds of Patriots
Book Four: The Journey Home
Book Five: Fortune in Men's Eyes
Book Six: The Debt
Book Seven: A Splendid Little War
Book Eight: A Test of Loyalty

Cover illustrator: Sara Boore

An American Family is a trademark of Fearon/Janus/Quercus.
Copyright © 1989 by Fearon/Janus/Quercus, a division of Simon &
Schuster Supplementary Education Group, 500 Harbor Boulevard,
Belmont, California 94002. All rights reserved. No part of this book
may be reproduced by any means, transmitted, or translated into a
machine language without the written permission of the publisher.

ISBN 0−8224−4754−1

Library of Congress Catalog Card Number: 88−81523

Printed in the United States of America.

10 9 8 7 6 5

Contents

FAMILY TREE

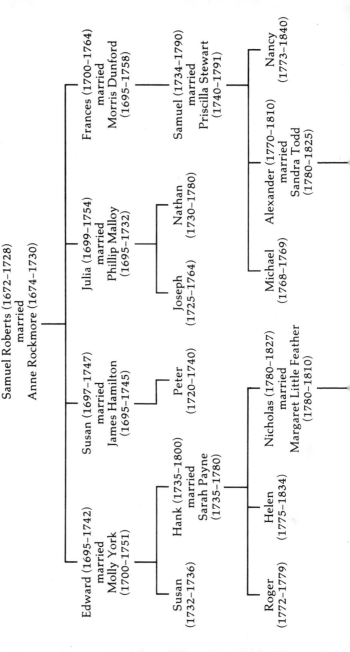

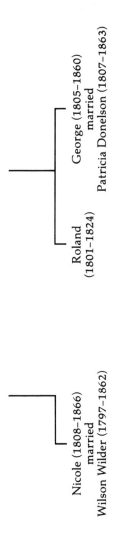

George (1805–1860)
married
Patricia Donelson (1807–1863)

Roland
(1801–1824)

Nicole (1808–1866)
married
Wilson Wilder (1797–1862)

The Missionary Orphanage

"My father had royal blood," Cecilia boasted. "In fact, if the family had stayed in Spain he would have been a count himself."

"You can't know that for sure," said Martha Sue. "Something that didn't really happen doesn't count. Now, *my* mother was truly, *in real life*, the most beautiful woman in St. Louis."

"Oh, come now, Martha Sue!" Cecilia snapped. "Perhaps you and your father thought so. But *really*—how can you be sure that others did too? Why, I've seen that painting of her. She was surely pretty enough, but—"

"Cecilia! Don't you speak of my mother that way!" Martha Sue cried.

Nicole Roberts set down her sewing. She was so painfully shy she almost never spoke in groups. But she couldn't stand this conversation any longer. "Would you two please stop quibbling about your parents? Talking about memories is one thing, but if you all have to—"

"Nicole!" Mrs. Saunderson rapped sharply on the wall with her gnarled fist. "Your tone of voice is most unpleasant."

Nicole's hands shook as she picked up her sewing again. She should know better than to talk out of turn. Still, Mrs. Saunderson never scolded the other young women. At least she didn't scold them as often as she did Nicole.

Very sweetly, Cecilia said, "Perhaps you could tell us about *your* father, Nicole. After all, he is still living."

Nicole felt as if Cecilia had stabbed her with a knife. Nothing shamed Nicole more than the fact that she was the only girl at the St. Louis Missionary Orphanage who had a living parent. She couldn't make up glamorous stories like the other girls.

The facts were plain: her father was alive. He was a fur trapper, and lived somewhere in the wild Rocky Mountains. Everyone knew that the fur trappers, who often came to St. Louis for supplies, were rough, mean-tempered men. They dressed like Indians and wore their hair long. They weren't the kind of men you'd be proud to show off.

Nicole's father not only *dressed* like an Indian, he had married one. Her mother had been a member of the Crow tribe from the Yellowstone River region.

Nicole used to ask questions about her parents. But the missionary couple who ran the orphanage claimed to know little about her past. Mr. and Mrs. Saunderson's silent disapproval made her imagine terrible things about her parents.

This much Nicole did know. She had been born in the Yellowstone River region in the heart of the Rocky Mountains. Her mother had died in 1810, when Nicole was two years old. Her father, somehow, had brought her down the Missouri to this St. Louis school for homeless girls. Since that time, she remembered seeing her father only two times. And she never had seen him alone.

His first visit was on her fourth birthday. Her father, Nicholas Roberts, arrived wearing a long-fringed buckskin jacket. His hair fell in a long braid down his back, and he smelled of tobacco.

Nicole remembered that day so well it might have been yesterday. Nicholas Roberts grinned widely at his daughter and opened his arms to her. But Nicole had already been taught to hate all that he was. She drew back with disgust crying, "Get away!" She would never forget the look on Mrs. Saunderson's face at that moment. The woman had nodded to Nicole ever so slightly, as if to say, "That's right. He *is* disgusting."

In the next moment, the child changed her mind about her father. Nicholas Roberts opened his big leather satchel. He pulled out a small Indian dress decorated with beads and feathers. Nicole had never seen a more beautiful piece of clothing. The little girl's feelings for her father immediately changed to affection.

But Mrs. Saunderson was clearly angry. "I believe it's time for you to leave now," she told Nicholas. "You can understand how confusing it is for the child."

Nicole cried when her father left. She rushed to the window to watch him walk down the street. How well she remembered that slow, heavy walk. How grateful she was for that colorful dress!

When her father was out of sight, Nicole turned to find her new dress.

"Where is it?" she demanded.

"What?" Mrs. Saunderson asked.

"My *dress*."

"I've thrown it away, young lady. And you're not to speak of it again. It's made of dirty animal skins. Your father showed very poor judgment in bringing it."

Nicole felt her insides shatter like glass. She began screaming for her dress and stomping her feet. Even Mr. Saunderson could not calm her down. When she finally wore herself out, Nicole was made to stay in her room for the next two days. She got no desserts and could not talk to the other girls.

Nicholas Roberts didn't visit his daughter again for years. Nicole knew that the Saundersons had convinced him to stay away. When she asked about him, they said she couldn't expect him to come all the way down the Missouri just to see her.

When Nicholas did visit again, Nicole had just turned fourteen. Her father came right into the dining hall looking for her. Nicole thought she would die of embarrassment. At the table he didn't know when to say please and thank you. He ate his meat right off the end of his knife. And he smacked his lips so loudly that a passerby outside the building could have heard!

Certainly he must have seen the other girls giggling and jabbing elbows. Certainly he must have seen the horror in his own daughter's face each time he opened his mouth to speak. After all, these young women were trained to be *ladies*!

Then after dinner, in front of all the other girls, he presented Nicole with a package.

Inside Nicole found a frilly pink dress. The dress was pretty, but it was the size and style a ten-year-old might wear.

Holding up the small dress, Nicole felt a flood of emotions inside her. She hated the other girls for laughing and whispering. And she also hated her father for embarrassing her like this. But most of all, she hated the Saundersons for making her hate who her father was.

Nicole went to her father to thank him for the dress. She was old enough this time to see that he, too, was ashamed. "Thank you Daddy," Nicole said. She bent to kiss him on the cheek.

Mrs. Saunderson jumped to her feet and said, "Say goodbye to him now." She hadn't said, "Say goodbye to your father." She'd said, "to *him*."

As Nicholas Roberts left this time, Nicole heard him mutter sheepishly to the Saundersons, "I reckon you folks think I ain't fit for a father."

Each summer, though, Nicholas Roberts deposited a chunk of his fur profits in a bank account he'd opened in Nicole's name. She learned that he also donated sums to the orphanage now and then. In that way, it seemed, he hoped to provide for his daughter the best he could.

Now in 1827, at the age of 19, Nicole owned a large savings account. But she had nothing to spend it on, and nowhere to go. So, though she was old enough to leave the orphanage, she stayed on as a teacher.

A month ago one young man had asked Nicole to marry him. Andrew Roscoe was a young missionary. He planned to go up the Missouri to "work with the Yellowstone Indians." But it was plain enough to Nicole that his proposal had nothing to do with love. He thought her Indian blood might help clear the way for his missionary work.

"You couldn't have hoped for better," Mrs. Saunderson told Nicole after Andrew made his proposal.

"Really, it's for the best," said the kinder Mr. Saunderson.

Nicole knew she had little choice. She didn't want to go on teaching at the orphanage forever. But Andrew Roscoe did not appeal to her one bit. He was a short, stocky man with curly blond hair. His eyes were a dull blue, though he tried to force a fiery expression into them. Nicole supposed he thought a passionate appearance was suitable in a missionary.

The truth was, Andrew Roscoe made Nicole quite angry. He expected her to be grateful to marry him. Instead of *asking* her, he had announced to her that they would marry. Then there was that self-satisfied look he wore so often. Oh, how awful it would be to spend a life with him!

Besides, Nicole wasn't interested in getting married. What she really wanted was to write a book. Mr. Saunderson had granted her special permission to visit the St. Louis Library each week. There, Nicole was making her way through as many books as she could.

Nicole could read much better than Mrs. Saunderson. Mr. Saunderson had her teach all the reading and writing classes to the younger girls. She knew that made Mrs. Saunderson angry. That's why, Nicole thought, Mrs. Saunderson always treated her so unkindly.

A few minutes after Mrs. Saunderson had scolded her, the woman marched over to Nicole's sewing table. She took the skirt out of Nicole's hands and held it up to the window. "Child, some of your stiches are an inch long! Will you never learn the most simple skills of sewing!"

Mrs. Saunderson took her small sewing scissors and cut out each of Nicole's stitches. She then dropped the cloth in Nicole's lap. "Begin again," she ordered. "Certainly the time you spend in the library would be better used practicing your stitching."

"I'll help her!" piped in Cecilia, smiling much too sweetly.

"That's good of you," Mrs. Saunderson said with a smug nod of her head.

Nicole decided right then to marry Andrew Roscoe. She realized that she would do anything—anything—to get away from the orphanage.

A Dying Man's Request

The sound of heavy boots pounding down the hallway drifted into the sewing room. All the young women looked up from their projects. Mrs. Saunderson went to the door just as it swung open, nearly knocking her over.

"I want to talk to Nicole Roberts!" boomed a deep-voiced man who was dressed as a trapper.

Mr. Saunderson, looking very irritated, followed the man into the room. "I told you, we will handle this. You have no right to interfere with the girl's life. You must leave immediately."

Nicole, still upset from Mrs. Saunderson's treatment of her, stood and walked to the man.

"Sit down young lady," ordered Mrs. Saunderson.

"I am Nicole Roberts," she told the young trapper.

"I need to speak to you in private, if I may," he said. Suddenly the man seemed shy, standing in front of Nicole.

"You may *not*," Mrs. Saunderson answered hotly.

"It's about your father," the man said to Nicole, ignoring Mrs. Saunderson.

Mrs. Saunderson placed herself between Nicole and the man.

"Oh, let me be!" cried Nicole. How tired she was of being treated like a child! She saw Mr. Saunderson hold back his wife as Nicole followed the man outside the door.

The man standing before Nicole was dressed much like her father, but he was many years younger. A leather band held his hair off his forehead. A knife hung at the waist of his pants. And he wore the mountain man's fringed buckskin jacket. He seemed as shy as Nicole herself. He pulled at the hat in his hands and kicked at the ground.

Somehow he was surprised at the girl's good looks. Nicole's eyes glistened a dark brown. Her skin too was a warm, tan shade. She wore her long black hair in a simple bun at the back of her neck. Nicole did not realize that she was strikingly beautiful. No one had ever told her.

"Uh . . . I have some . . . uh . . . bad news, Miss Roberts." The man coughed gently. "Your father and I have been partners for ten years. But . . . uh . . . he's dead now."

"Dead." Nicole tried to give the word meaning by speaking it aloud. Her father was *dead*. What did that mean? Who had he been anyway? Sadness overwhelmed Nicole. Not because she would miss him. But because she never knew him. "How?" she asked softly.

"Well, I'm not quite sure, Miss. He was one of the most reckless men I've ever met. I always figured he'd get killed doing something foolish. But the way it was, he just took a fever. He knew he was going. He said,

'Wilson, I'm going. Go fetch my daughter Nicole and do whatever you can for her. I did the best I could for that girl. But I never got over leaving her with them missionaries. Still I couldn't see any other choice, when her mother died. The Crow would have raised her, sure enough. But after that Meriwether Lewis problem, I just didn't know.'"

The trapper paused self-consciously. Then he explained. "See, Meriwether Lewis shot a Blackfoot brave in 1806, just two years before you were born. The Blackfeet never forgave him. They blamed all white men, especially the trappers. So Nick was thinking that if the Blackfeet got into something with the Crow, then, well, a half-white baby girl might get hurt."

Nicole nodded slowly, feeling lost and terribly alone. "What's your name?" she asked.

"I'm Wilson Wilder. Excuse me, Miss, for forgetting to tell you. Anyway, your pa told me you have quite a heap of money in the bank here. He wanted me to remind you of that. All the time I knew him, Miss, he fretted over you."

"He did?"

"Yes, Miss. He was never sure if he did the right thing by bringing you here. He sometimes thought of coming to get you out. But what would a school-trained girl do in the bush? He brought you downriver to St. Louis when you were two. He was grief-stricken by the loss of his wife. How was he going to raise a baby girl and trap at the same time? But as I say, he never knew whether he made the right choice.

"Anyway, he instructed me on a few things. One was to let you know you weren't forgotten. Two, was to tell you about your money. And three, well, I'm supposed to help you out in any way I can. You just tell me what you need, Miss."

Nicole couldn't speak. So many things were going through her head. Then Wilson Wilder continued. "Your cousin from Carolina, Roland Dunford, trapped with your pa and me for a couple of years. His folks sent him out West. I guess he was a disgrace to the family. He just couldn't cut it with those genteel southern folk. Anyway, as your pa was dying he said that maybe you'd like to go down to live on the plantation with them. They owe his side of the family a favor. Of course, they may not see it that way. Not since Roland died in the arms of a grizzly near the Wind River. But—"

"Wait a minute," Nicole said.

"Excuse me, Miss. I guess there was so much to tell you that I was just running at the mouth. I'll be in town for a few days restocking. I'll come back." Then he turned and walked off.

That evening Nicole's mind was whirling. She couldn't imagine taking any of her three choices. Staying at the orphanage any longer seemed unbearable. Marrying Andrew Roscoe was worse. And she'd read in the paper about how Negroes were treated in the South. She didn't want to find out how they felt about a half-Indian.

"Nicole," Mr. Saunderson said after dinner. "Mr. Roscoe has learned of your loss. He thinks it's time to marry." Mr. Saunderson smiled carefully, knowing that it wasn't her favorite idea.

"You're a lucky girl," Mrs. Saunderson added. "All too lucky."

In a warmer voice, Mr. Saunderson said, "Really, Nicole, it's the best thing for you to do. Andrew is a fine young man. And as you know, he plans to go up the Missouri. Why, that might make a good topic for that book you want to write!"

Nicole smiled. She knew Mr. Saunderson was trying to be nice. And he did make one good point. Going West would give her a topic for a book. Perhaps she could return to the place of her birth, meet her family on her mother's side. But could she accept Andrew Roscoe as part of the deal?

A knock on the parlor door prompted Mrs. Saunderson to say, "There he is now."

"Who?" Nicole asked. "You don't mean Andrew!"

Mrs. Saunderson turned and gave Nicole a look as cold as stone. "Dear, your options are few. I suggest you take what comes your way."

As the woman answered the door, Mr. Saunderson patted Nicole's hand. "We want only the best for you, my dear. One day you shall see the wisdom of this decision."

"My dear Nicole," said Andrew Roscoe as he rushed into the room. "I am so sorry to hear of the death of your blood relation."

"My *father*," Nicole corrected. They all spoke of him as if he were a distant relative.

"Yes of course, your father. Well, have you all discussed our plans?"

"We have indeed!" cried Mrs. Saunderson forcefully.

"Good. I am sure, dear Nicole, that you shall be quite a helpmate to me in the wilderness. We have such a lot of work to do."

Andrew Roscoe began outlining his plans for 'civilizing' the Indians. He spoke as loudly as if he were addressing an entire hall of people. Mrs. Saunderson sat tall and nodded her head vigorously at each word. Nicole noticed that Mr. Saunderson nodded sleepily.

Finally, Nicole cut in. "Excuse me," she said quietly. Andrew stopped and frowned at her. He was annoyed at having been interrupted. "I have indeed been *told* of your plans, but I have not agreed," Nicole said firmly. "I shall need a day or two to think on it. Good night."

As she left the room, she glanced at Andrew. His face had nearly turned purple. A dull anger clouded his eyes. He did not like the idea of Nicole telling him maybe. A gentler man, she thought, might understand her misgivings.

The next day the Saundersons jumped on her once again. "Nicole, the wilderness will certainly be a challenge, but you will not live there forever. And—"

"I'm not at all afraid to go into the wilderness," Nicole replied. "It's Andrew Roscoe I cannot bear. I've made my decision. I plan on going up the Missouri, all right. But I'm going with Mr. Wilson Wilder, not Andrew Roscoe."

Mrs. Saunderson laughed rudely. "Why, he's half-animal! Child, you have lost your mind altogether." She turned to Mr. Saunderson. "I told you the girl was reading too much."

"What about the book you want to write!" cried Mr. Saunderson. "Does Wilson Wilder know of this idea?"

"No, but my father asked him to do my bidding. This is my bidding. For as you yourself pointed out, the adventure would make a very good book."

That afternoon Nicole told Wilson of her wish to return to her birthplace.

"Miss Roberts, that's impossible! There's nothing for you out there. What would you do? Who would you stay with? Impossible. The idea is impossible."

"You told me my father asked you—*on his deathbed*—to do as I wished," Nicole replied. She felt a little awkward. She was not the sort of woman to force people into things. But she felt desperate.

Wilson shook his head and laughed shyly. "A book-learned woman in Yellowstone country! You have your father's reckless character, all right!"

However, Wilson Wilder did not take promises lightly. Nicholas Roberts had been more than his best friend. He'd taught the younger man everything he knew about trapping.

Wilson had an idea. A businessman named Daniel Zimmer planned to take a keelboat up the Missouri this week. He had offered to pay Wilson handsomely to guide his group to the Yellowstone River. Zimmer hoped to stay in the West and open a fort. He wanted to cash in on the fur trade. A pair of botanists would be on the expedition, too. They, and some of the crew, would return with the keelboat before winter set in.

Normally Wilson would slip up the Missouri in his canoe. But if he joined Zimmer's expedition, he could make a little easy money. He would tell Zimmer that Nicole's passage was part of the deal. Wilson felt quite sure that Nicole would be ready to return when the botanists did. Then Wilson could remain in the Rockies.

So it was settled. Nicole sent a note to Andrew Roscoe. Being as kind as possible, she told him she could not marry him. She did not tell him of her plans.

The Big Muddy

It was easy to see why people called the Missouri River the Big Muddy. "It's too thick to drink and too thin to plow," Wilson Wilder said. Nicole now stood on the bank next to the keelboat.

The night before, Mrs. Saunderson's parting words to Nicole had been, "We have failed. If this gets around St. Louis, no one will trust their youngsters to us."

Mr. Saunderson also shook his head sadly at her. But then he quietly placed a book of poetry in Nicole's hands. "God be with you," he said warmly.

Nicole knew this was an odd plan for a woman of nineteen. She was going into the wilds with a man she'd known for only a week! Now she glanced sideways at Wilson Wilder. He held a long rifle. A butcher knife, stuck in a sheath of buffalo hide, hung from his belt. This man was a far cry from the young men the Saundersons brought to tea after church.

Nicole took note of the other men on the keelboat. The expedition leader, Daniel Zimmer, was decidedly handsome. And the university botanists seemed quite interesting. Just now they were putting together a trunk full of trowels, little hammers, and specimen boxes. Nicole watched the crew members ready the oars and poles.

Then a final passenger walked briskly up the dock. Nicole thought she would faint. It was Andrew Roscoe.

He spotted her right away. To her horror she saw his face light up. He walked swiftly to her side.

"So you have changed your mind, I see. A rather sudden turn of events, but so like women! And while I'm not entirely pleased, I shall yield.

"However, I understand the boat leaves in a few hours. If you think we might marry somewhere along the way, you are mistaken. Come, we must hurry. I am sure the Reverend Saunderson will be more than pleased to do the honors."

Nicole was speechless. Before she could get a word out, Wilson called, "Miss Roberts! Stash your trunk. It's in the crew's way."

"Who's that?" Andrew demanded.

"Andrew, I have not changed my mind," Nicole said. "Our meeting is quite by accident. I am going to the Yellowstone River, accompanied by my father's partner, Mr. Wilson Wilder. I plan to . . . uh . . . meet my family, visit my birthplace, and take notes for a book."

Never had Nicole seen a face look so dark. Embarrassment and hatred swirled in Andrew's eyes. She dreaded the weeks aboard the keelboat with him. He turned and stormed back to his cabin.

Two hours later the crew slipped their long poles into the water. They began pushing the keelboat up the Missouri against the strong current. In her excitement Nicole forgot about Andrew Roscoe.

For three days, Nicole stood on deck and watched the fine prairies roll by. It seemed the whole countryside was teeming with wild plums and apples, gooseberries and raspberries.

Andrew treated her with icy politeness. He clearly thought she was a disgrace. But Nicole was not about to let him ruin her trip. She was having the time of her life.

On the fourth day, they reached a place where the river split into two streams. The channel to the right looked much deeper and clearer. To the left there was a tangle of snags and upended logs.

"Go to the left," Wilson ordered. "It's all quicksand around the bend to the right."

"Not on your life," answered Daniel Zimmer. "Any fool can see the snags. It's clear and free-flowing to the right."

"Daniel," Wilson said. "I've been up this river many times."

Andrew Roscoe stepped up, his dull eyes narrowed at Wilson. "A man simply needs a pair of eyes to see which way to go."

"To the right!" Zimmer ordered the crew.

Wilson lit his pipe and took a seat. He watched the men guide the boat round the bend. In a few minutes, the keelboat slid neatly into the thick quicksand.

"Push!" Zimmer yelled at the men with the poles. "Harder! Get us out of here."

As each moment passed, Wilson knew that the boat was becoming more tightly wedged in. But he said nothing. He just waited—to teach Zimmer a lesson. Wilson felt if he was going to go up the Missouri with these fools, *he* was going to be in charge. He didn't have time for this kind of stupidity.

An hour later Zimmer said, "Wilder! I paid you good money to guide us. What should we do?"

Wilson looked up from his pipe as if he had just noticed they were stuck. "Get some men ashore with two ropes. Haul the boat back downstream." Then Wilson jumped up and good-naturedly took charge.

The following week the botanists went ashore to collect samples. When they didn't return, Wilson went ashore to search for them. Three hours later he came back. He was nearly dragging the university fellows by their collars.

Then came the last straw. Daniel Zimmer aimed his gun at a group of Indians who'd come to the shore to trade. Wilson knocked the gun out of his hands. "Are you crazy?" he shouted. "These men have come to offer you food, and you point your gun at them?"

"You can never be too careful," Zimmer responded.

Wilson took a deep breath. "Look. If you are afraid of someone and point your gun at him, you only set up a fight. It's simple. If you want to be on friendly terms with the Indians, show some good will."

When Wilson saw that Zimmer wouldn't take his advice, he decided he'd had enough. The next morning Wilson unloaded his canoe off the keelboat. He threw his bags overboard into the canoe. Zimmer and the rest of the crew rushed up on deck.

"I'm sorry," Wilson said. "But you've been averaging less than eight miles a day. At this rate, I'll miss a lot of fall trapping. I have to leave. Here's all of the advance payment you gave me."

Nicole was the first to speak. "You can't be serious! You promised my father . . ." Her voice trailed off.

Andrew Roscoe stepped up beside her. "What did you expect from him, anyway?" he snorted.

"You're not going anywhere," Zimmer said to Wilson in a low, gravelly voice. "An agreement is an agreement."

"I told you I'd guide you up the Missouri to the Yellowstone *in time for fall trapping,*" Wilson replied. "Your part of the deal was to provide a responsible crew. We've lost whole days because of your poor navigation and bad decisions."

"What about the lady?" asked Andrew Roscoe, as if it was his business.

"That's right," Zimmer said. "Don't think we'll cart her up the Missouri for you. She's part of *your* baggage."

Baggage! Nicole had never felt so humiliated. Andrew looked so smug. He took her arm. "Never mind," he said in a voice much deeper than his usual one. "I'll be responsible for the lady."

Wilson swung overboard and into his canoe. He knelt and began arranging his things. He wouldn't look at Nicole.

"Oh, no you don't!" Nicole cried, fear blowing away her shyness. She yanked her arm away from Andrew. Then she swung herself overboard and into Wilson's canoe. "You should be ashamed. Leaving your recently dead partner's daughter with a bunch of bumblers."

"What's that you called us, lady?" Zimmer shouted.

Nicole ignored Zimmer and continued talking to Wilson. "You are the only one aboard who has the slightest hint of how to manage in the wilderness. Deserting me would be as good as killing me."

"Miss Roberts," Wilson said, with a desperate tone in his voice. "You don't understand. I will paddle my canoe up the Missouri and begin trapping soon. I couldn't possibly take you along. What would you do? It will be several months before I'd come to the home of the Crow on the Yellowstone River."

"Mr. Wilder, you *promised* my father you would grant my wish. You might have said earlier that you wouldn't take me. But now that we've come this far, you cannot leave me with these men. They consider me your 'baggage'!"

Wilson felt ashamed and worried. He knew so little about women. What had possessed him to let her come this far? Now he was stuck. He knew he couldn't leave her with Zimmer. But what would he do with a soft-spoken, book-learned lady in the woods. Oh, how had he gotten into this mess?

Just then Nicole heard a rifle being cocked. Zimmer aimed it at Wilson's head. "Get back on board, son," he said. "And if you think I'd hesitate to blow your head off, you're mistaken. We got a crew of 20 here. And let me tell you something. I'll give any of these men $100 if they catch you trying to sneak off. Come on, pull your canoe back on board."

Wilson gave the group of men a long, cool look. "Well, if you put it that way," he said with a smile. "Give me a hand there, Andrew, will you?" Wilson tossed his heavy bag of beaver traps at Andrew. The young man fell on his back trying to catch it.

So the trip down the Big Muddy continued. Two nights later Wilson shook Nicole awake. He told her to keep perfectly quiet and get dressed. Going up on deck, Nicole saw his canoe, once again bobbing in the water. She climbed in after Wilson. In the light of a full moon, they began slipping downstream.

"Where are we going?" she asked, afraid of the answer.

"I'm taking you home," he said.

"No," Nicole responded. She thought of how self-satisfied Mrs. Saunderson would look if she returned. Again she said, "No!"

Then she realized there was more at stake than just facing Mrs. Saunderson again. "Wilson" she said. "I want to see the country where my parents lived. I want to see where I was born. If I have to walk there alone, I will. Just set me off on the riverbank."

Wilson watched her earnest face as she spoke. The moonlight shone in her eyes. He pulled the oar out of the water.

"Besides," Nicole added. "If you take me home now, you shall miss *all* of the fall trapping."

Wilson didn't exactly smile. But Nicole saw a warm look spread across his face. In one graceful motion, he swung the canoe around. As easy as a salmon, Nicole thought. The canoe moved swiftly up the Missouri River.

Alone with a Mountain Man

Nicole had left her trunk on the keelboat. But she had managed to bring along a small bag. In it she'd thrown a change of clothes, two writing notebooks, and the volume of poetry Mr. Saunderson gave her.

In the silver light of the full moon, Wilson paddled swiftly and silently up the Missouri. He seemed relieved to be in his canoe again. Now they wouldn't have to worry about snags and quicksand.

Nicole sat facing Wilson. She couldn't help but stare at him. He really wasn't so bad-looking, after all. His eyes were expressive and kind. And though his nose was some-what large and crooked, his brow stood out handsomely. She would have trouble, though, getting used to the long braid down his back.

Wilson rowed expertly through the night and the next day. They hardly exchanged a handful of words. Nicole was still angry with him for planning to desert her. At the same time, she realized what a burden she would be. Nicole did her best not to look as tired as she felt.

Sometimes, she caught Wilson stealing glances at her. Once she tried to smile, but he quickly looked away.

"There's no chance they could catch us now," Wilson finally said. "But I'd just as soon put some miles between them and us. We're making pretty good time, too." Then he added, "In 1810 John Colter paddled from the Missouri's source to St. Louis in a month."

"How did my father get *me* down the Missouri?" Nicole asked.

"You never heard that story?" Wilson looked surprised. "Why, everyone west of the Mississippi knows it by heart. But now that I think about it, I guess you *wouldn't* have heard it."

Wilson stretched out his legs without missing a beat in his rowing. "Nick—that's your pa—came West on the heels of Meriwether Lewis and William Clark. Those are the fellows President Jefferson sent to explore the Louisiana Purchase. That was in 1806. The next year Nick came up the Missouri with a businessman named Manuel Lisa. He left Lisa's company right away, though. Nick was the best trapper around. Why should he pay Lisa part of his profits?

"Anyway, that fall Nick married a Crow woman. You were born the following year.

"Then, just two years after that, your mother died. To hear Nick talk about it, you'd think she died yesterday. He just never got over her."

Nicole was fascinated. How often she'd longed to know the details of her past! She knew now that she made the right decision in taking this journey.

Wilson continued, "So he wrapped you up and paddled you down the Missouri. I wish you could have heard your father tell it. He sure could turn a good story. There he was, a big, gruff, mountain man with a two-year-old baby girl. Nick had friends in every tribe along the way, so he got lots of help. Women were eager to give you milk and give Nick advice. Some women even offered to adopt you. But Nick decided you were going to become book-learned. Also, I think he figured he could keep better track of you in an orphanage.

"Every time Nick told the story, he ended by saying. 'Maybe I made a mistake. Maybe I should have made her the first girl trapper. What do you think, Wilson?' I'd always answer, 'Naw, Nick. What about the blizzards in the dead of winter? A baby has to be fed and held. What would you do with her while you were checking your traps?'

"Then Nick would always take out his pipe and look into the fire for a long time. He just never quite settled it in his own mind—about your mother dying and his taking you to live in that orphanage with the missionaries."

The days passed quickly as they paddled up the Missouri. In the evenings, Nicole tried to make herself as useful as possible. She helped gather firewood and learned to build fires.

Then each night after supper, the two of them sat by the fire. Nicole wrote the day's events and sights into one of her notebooks. Wilson mended his traps and sharpened his knife.

Since the nights were still warm, they slept under the stars. Out of courtesy to Nicole, Wilson always carried his blankets a good distance from the fire. Nicole wrapped up cozily next to the coals.

In spite of the discomfort, Nicole was enjoying herself. She loved lying under the stars at night. She loved the wide freedom of the outdoors. She'd never known happier moments than those few before she fell into a deep sleep.

One night by the campfire, Wilson surprised Nicole by pulling out a book. A trapper with a book? She couldn't believe it. "What have you got there?" she asked.

"Oh, just a bit of poetry."

"And who is the author?" Nicole asked, figuring it was some mountain poet.

"Let's see," Wilson looked at the cover of the book and frowned a little. Then he winked at her. "Some fellow calls himself Shakespeare."

"Shakespeare! You're reading Shake-speare?"

"So you've heard of him?"

"Now you're making fun of me," Nicole said. "I just never knew that trappers, well—"

"Read," Wilson finished the sentence for her. He smiled. "I guess we aren't a group known for our love of literature. But Nick was a big reader. That's why he wanted you to be book-learned. He hoped you'd be a writer some day."

"He did?"

"Yep." Wilson turned the volume of Shake-speare over in his hands. "This here was his favorite book. That's why I kept it. He often read out loud at night."

Wilson looked sad now. He certainly painted a different picture of her father than the Saundersons had.

Then Wilson grinned again. "When he wasn't reading stories, he was telling them out of his head. All about that crazy family of yours."

"What do you mean crazy? What kind of stories?"

"Oh, there was Nick's great grandfather—your great-great-grandfather—who was tried for witchcraft. Then there were these Carolina cousins. They were wild seagoing types. And there was an aunt of his who made herself a fortune in rice. He said she worked right alongside slaves in the fields. Oh, and certainly you would have heard about your grandfather and his cousin. Then again, maybe you wouldn't have. Those two men met as soldiers in the War for Independence. Honored by George Washington himself, both of them.

"Oh, your father could go on for hours with stories," Wilson continued. "I suspected he made up a lot of those things about your family, but I never let on."

Nicole learned that her father was famous all up and down the Missouri. Wilson seemed to know everyone they saw, and he always introduced her as Nick Roberts's daughter. Nicole would see respect wash over the people's faces. The Indians usually gave her presents. The white trappers told her stories about what a fine man Nick was.

Nicole wished she could return to St. Louis for just a few moments. She would proudly tell Cecilia and Martha Sue that her father was one of the first white trappers in the West. She would boast that his name is known and respected in a region far greater than the size of St. Louis!

One night Wilson cut up a leather hide. Next he sewed the pieces together with small, fine stitches. Nicole laughed at the thought that Mrs. Saunderson wouldn't have torn out *his* stitches. In three evenings Wilson had made a fine pair of buckskin pants.

"Aren't those rather small?" Nicole looked first at Wilson, then the pants.

"They're for you," he answered. "Soon we'll be leaving the river and traveling overland, through the brush. You'll never make it in all that garb you've been wearing."

Trapping for Beaver

It was time to move inland. Wilson stashed his canoe in a place he could find later. Then he bought three horses from some Sioux Indians. He and Nicole left the Big Muddy. They set out overland, heading West.

Wearing her buckskin trousers, Nicole quickly learned to ride a horse. She missed the soft, rippling sound of the canoe slipping through the water. But she loved the rush of wind in the trees, the flapping of birds' wings overhead, the crunch of the horses' hooves on the forest floor.

Yet Nicole grew worried. She noticed a cold snap in the morning air. The aspen leaves had begun to turn a lovely gold. One morning she awoke to see that her breath had turned to ice on her blanket. "Wilson," she called to him as he built up the fire. "Will we make it to the country of the Crow people by winter?"

Wilson looked up surprised. "Oh, you wouldn't want to winter in the Rockies."

"You said we were going to Yellowstone country!"

"We don't have enough time to get there."

"Well, what am I going to do?" she cried, sitting up in her bedroll. "Am I supposed to spend the winter in the wilds with a man I hardly know?"

"Miss Roberts," Wilson said, his mouth forming a tight line. "This was *your* idea, not mine. I assure you that I would get along much better without you."

The words felt like blows to Nicole. Yet she knew that Wilson was simply being frank and truthful. To him, she was his best friend's daughter, someone he felt indebted to. And of course he was right. He had warned her, and tried to take her home.

"And besides," Wilson said, trying to soften his harsh words. "If I miss fall trapping, I won't be able to buy supplies next year."

Nicole bit her lip. She wished, just a little, that Wilson looked on her as something more than an obligation. But then she thought about the orphanage. She figured that nothing was more unbearable than spending the winter months in the sewing room with Cecilia and Martha Sue. She was determined to see herself through this winter in the wilds. And she would not be a burden to Wilson Wilder.

So each day Nicole tried to help more. She learned to pack the horses. She even learned to notice signs of game. At first she couldn't understand how Wilson did it. All of a sudden he'd stop dead still. She could almost see his ears prick up, like an animal's. Moments later, a flock of geese would fly overhead. Or a deer would cross their path. Nicole didn't understand how he could hear and see things before they were there.

"What is it?" she had cried foolishly the first couple of times she saw him stop. The sound of her voice scared the game away. But Nicole soon learned to stop as suddenly and quietly as Wilson. She began to notice signs of game herself, like trampled grass or the sudden flight of birds. Sometimes Nicole noticed something before Wilson did. Then *she* would stop instantly and hold up *her* hand to silence Wilson. How she loved those times! Wilson, too, would grin.

Once Wilson caught a fox because of her. After skinning it, he said, "This one's for you. It'll draw a good price. You can add it to your savings."

Nicole smiled broadly.

"Miss Roberts?" Wilson said looking embarrassed. "Do you mind if I speak plainly with you?"

"That won't be anything new," she teased.

"What do you intend to do with the money your father left you?"

"I haven't really thought about it."

"I'd like to give you a little advice, if I may."

"Of course."

"You're a very bright woman. But you're a bit innocent. You've been sheltered, if I may say so. I'm afraid you might stumble into an uncomfortable situation sometime. You have a way of, well, striking out rather blindly."

Nicole didn't like this speech. But she recognized the truth of what he was saying. So she listened.

"Your father was an excellent trapper. And he got started early—when there were still fortunes to be made. Besides that, he didn't drink or gamble. That means there's a lot of money in your bank account."

Wilson looked at his hands. "You're kind of a legend in these parts. Everybody knows the story of how Nick Roberts paddled his baby girl down the Missouri. So, well—they might guess about your money, too.

"Shoot, what I'm trying to say is that most trappers are good and honest men. But there are a few bad apples out there. And I don't want you falling into the wrong hands."

"I'm not insulted at you calling me innocent," Nicole replied. "I know I am. But it doesn't take much worldly experience to tell a good apple from a bad apple, Wilson. That much I'm quite good at, thank you."

"Uh, yes. I'm sorry if I said the wrong thing." Wilson looked as if he might choke. Quickly he picked up his gun and disappeared in the forest.

Nicole watched him go and wondered. If Wilson really believed she couldn't look after herself, she'd be angry. But she sensed some other concern behind his words. It was almost as if he didn't like the idea of men being interested in her. That, of course, was silly. He'd probably like nothing better than for some other trapper to take her off his hands. Maybe that's why he mentioned it. He wanted her to be on the lookout for a husband.

Their journey went on. They traveled less and less each day as Wilson hunted more. He hunted game for dinner and fur for profit. He caught a few wolves and raccoon for their hides. But he grew frustrated in not finding any beaver.

Then one day they happened upon a huge dam. Wilson searched the area to make sure he wasn't on another trapper's territory. Then he carefully took out six traps from his trap sack.

Nicole studied his every move so she could help the next time. First he found six good sticks and sharpened one end of each. Then he waded out in the icy water near the dam. He set the triggers on the traps. And he secured them by driving the sharpened sticks into the streambed.

Next Wilson waded back to shore and found a willow twig. He dipped the twig in the antelope horn at his belt. "Medicine," he said winking at Nicole. Then he added, "That's what we call bait. Beavers like the scent." He placed a bait twig over each of six traps.

The next morning Nicole and Wilson found six fat beavers. Wilson skinned the beavers by the shore. He saved the special glands that contained the "medicine" used to bait the traps.

Wilson showed Nicole how to clean the skins. Then he made large hoops out of willow branches. Finally the skins were stretched onto the willow hoops and set out to dry.

That night as Nicole gathered wood, Wilson built a roaring fire. When she returned with the last armload, he was arranging a fat beaver tail on the coals.

If there had been anything in Nicole's stomach, it would have come up right then. She'd eaten many disgusting things on this trip, but charred beaver tail was the limit.

"Just wait," Wilson said, reading her face. "You'll love it. After charring, I'll boil it. We call this trapper's caviar!"

Wilson was in a great mood. Six beavers in one day was quite a start to the season. Nicole knew he was disappointed that she wouldn't touch the beaver tail. He unpacked some dried venison for her supper. After he'd had his fill of beaver tail, he smoked his pipe.

"Miss Roberts?" He said it so shyly, Nicole had to smile. "Would you mind reading to me a bit? I do miss hearing your father read."

Nicole wondered why he hadn't asked sooner. She found the book of poetry Mr.

Saunderson had given her. As she read, she realized how warm and pleasant the words sounded when spoken out loud. Before she knew it, she'd read half the poems in the book.

She looked up. The expression on Wilson's face amazed her. He looked dazed, faraway, and gentle. Here was a wild and rough mountain man. Yet he seemed to enjoy poetry more than anyone she'd ever known. She'd also noticed how he seemed to hear music in the trees and rivers. Nicole couldn't help comparing him to the sort of men the Saundersons used to parade in to tea. For all their training and manners, none of them seemed as refined as Wilson did right now.

"Why did you stop reading?" Wilson asked. The firelight danced across his face, picking up a brightness in his eyes.

"Oh, I'm sorry," she said, embarrassed for staring at him. She continued reading late into the night. Her voice became hoarse and scratchy, but she didn't stop until she'd read the entire volume.

Nicole's wilderness education continued. She learned to make willow hoops, and to clean, and stretch the animal hides. "You're a natural," Wilson told her.

"My ancestors," Nicole answered smiling. "Look where all that embroidery and lessons in manners got me."

Often Wilson seemed pleased with her. Nicole could almost believe she was more of a help than a nuisance. She certainly *felt* more useful cleaning and stretching hides than she had ever felt sewing tiny stitches on ugly dresses. And the setting for her work! Instead of the drab green walls of the orphanage, she looked up at sheer rock bluffs. There was beauty all around her. She heard the clear river water splash and tumble by and she saw the trees blazing red, orange, and yellow.

One sunny morning Nicole sat happily preparing willow hoops. She chuckled as she watched Wilson leave to check his traps. The night before she'd tried eating a bit of beaver tail. She delighted Wilson by admitting that it was quite tasty.

No sooner was Wilson out of sight, than something rustled in the trees behind her. Nicole set down her work. Clearly this was not a raccoon or even a deer. It sounded bigger. Much bigger.

Nicole turned, slowly and without making a sound, to look toward the noise. At first she could see nothing because the rising sun was shining in her eyes. Then the creature rose up in front of the sun. It was an enormous grizzly bear.

The bear stood at least six-feet tall. Its coat was dark brown with light brown, almost silvery, highlights. Its long curled claws hung from giant padded feet. The grizzly's open mouth showed great yellow teeth. Nicole could hear the huge beast's heavy raspy breathing.

Still on its hind legs, the bear tried to take a step toward her. Suddenly it fell to its four feet and lumbered closer.

Nicole wanted to sit on the ground and scream for dear life. But she forced herself not to.

"Go away!" she told the grizzly as sternly as she could, as if the huge bear were a pesky dog. "Scat now."

The bear took a few more steps toward her.

Nicole reached for Wilson's gun. She pointed it at the bear and looked through the viewer. She saw the bear stand on its hind legs again, and she put her finger on the trigger. Through the viewer she saw the bear open its huge mouth as if ready to sink its teeth into something. But it was only yawning. As if bored, the bear swung around and began waddling away.

Just then Nicole heard the clanging of Wilson's traps.

"Miss Roberts!" he shouted as he ran into camp. The back end of the grizzly was just disappearing into the woods.

Nicole lowered the gun. "For goodness sakes, Wilson," she said, relief flooding her senses. "Don't you think it's about time you called me 'Nicole'?"

Wilson looked at her like she'd gone completely mad. He held his head and leaned against a tree. As if *he'd* been the one in a showdown with a grizzly! He shook himself and asked, "Are you okay, Miss, uh, Nicole?"

She smiled at his concern. "I'm fine. Really. I kept my head the whole time. Until this minute, anyway. Right now I feel about ready to collapse!"

Wilson walked quickly to her side. He reached out and touched her arm. But he quickly withdrew his hand. "I'm so glad you're all right," he said. Then he repeated her name, "Nicole."

In the Shadow of the Rockies

Each week the snow moved farther down the mountains. Winter was upon them. The streams began to ice over, putting an end to beaver trapping. Wilson chose a site with trees for shelter and a clear running stream. In just two weeks he built a two-room cabin with a stone fireplace and a small barn for the horses.

Very impressed, Nicole asked, "Do you build a two-room cabin every winter?"

"Not quite like this," he said. "But I've never spent a winter with a lady." Wilson's face turned bright red.

Nicole thought it was funny that he still became embarrassed around her. After all, they'd camped together for months. A two-room cabin would give each of them more privacy than they'd had since their journey on the keelboat.

"I'm beginning to feel like a regular bear myself," she joked to Wilson. She made the comment to make him feel more comfortable.

But he got a funny look on his face and asked, "What do you mean?"

"I mean I could live like this forever," she said.

Wilson turned on his heel, grabbed his gun, and left the cabin. Then Nicole realized what she'd said. Why was she so stupid? How could she forget the burden she was to him? Just because she was enjoying the outdoors didn't mean he enjoyed having her along! She must tell him that she would return home as soon as possible.

Home? Nicole wasn't sure where that was. St. Louis hardly felt like home, anymore.

In any case, there was no going anywhere during the winter months. Wilson filled his days fixing the cabin. And he still hunted, even though they'd dried plenty of meat for eating.

Nicole still looked for any jobs she could do. She kept the cabin clean and searched for firewood each day. At night she would write in one of her notebooks. Sometimes she tried to cook, but Wilson was much better at that. Besides, he became grumpy when he didn't have something to do.

Nicole thought Wilson was a bit like a bear himself. During the winter months, he seemed to draw into himself. It was almost as if he were hibernating. He grew moody and talked less than he had before. Nicole felt perhaps he was growing tired of her. But sometimes at night they still talked and told stories.

"Tell me," she said one night. "You said a grizzly killed my cousin, Roland Dunford. How did that happen?"

Wilson laughed just at the mention of Roland's name. He lit his pipe before beginning. "Your cousin came out West in 1823. A Virginian gentleman named William Ashley came with him. As soon as he got on the

Missouri Roland began asking folks if they knew Nick Roberts. So we got reports of this boy long before we saw him. For a while Nick made a game of avoiding him. Someone would say, 'There's a young fellow up at so-and-so's fort looking for you.' Nick would say, 'We'd best get moving. We don't need no southern genteel to anchor us.'

"Roland finally found him. Truth was, I think Nick was genuinely pleased to meet up with some family folk. Roland was a round fellow with rosy cheeks. But he wasn't too quick on his feet. Nick pretended not to be interested for a spell. But soon those two were joking and doing such tomfoolery, I thought they were likely to get us *all* killed. I won't say I wasn't glad when Roland was off our hands. Your father was reckless some-times, but he was smart and he knew his business. Roland was just plain reckless.

"It was the time of year when the bears are particularly hungry." Wilson looked at Nicole and winced. He was thinking of her close call. "Roland had just shot a deer. He was skinning the animal when the bear came upon him. The bear lunged, hoping to scare Roland away from the meat. Roland foolishly tried to protect his catch. That bear made mincemeat of your cousin in two seconds flat."

Nicole nodded. Later, before falling off to sleep, she wondered if Wilson thought she had more sense than Roland. She hoped so.

Sometimes, on clear days, Nicole went for walks. Wilson made her a pair of snowshoes and she'd gotten very good at using them. She discovered a ridge that she could climb and catch a view of the Rockies.

She climbed that ridge dozens of times that winter. Each time the scenery from the top made her gasp as if she were seeing it for the first time. The massive white mountains rose up in striking beauty against the blue sky. To think her mother had lived her entire life in the shadow of such beauty!

Often, while standing on top of the ridge, Nicole practiced speeches she might give to Wilson. She wanted to tell him, "You have been kind to bring me this far. Grant me one more favor and you can wash your hands of me. When the ice breaks up in the spring, escort me to the Missouri River. With the funds my father left me, I am sure I can bribe some keelboat crew to take me home."

But Nicole wanted to go back to St. Louis about as much as she wanted to face that grizzly again. The mountains made her feel alive and strong. She loved the warmth of the cabin fire and the simplicity of Wilson's company. Funny how this wild country felt so much more like home than St. Louis. And she still had yet to see the Yellowstone country and meet the Crow Indians!

Even so, she couldn't continue to tie down Wilson. So every day she would walk back from the ridge full of determination. *Tonight* she would ask Wilson to escort her to the Missouri in the spring. But she could never bring herself to do it.

Sometimes during the day Nicole thought up stories to tell Wilson at night. They already had read all their books.

"All that in your head?" Wilson asked her one night. Nicole nodded. "You should write those stories down in your notebooks. You could sell them to magazines."

Nicole enjoyed the compliment at first. But the part about selling her stories made her sad. She was sure Wilson was hinting that she'd have to find a way to take care of herself. She opened her mouth to speak. She wanted to assure him that she'd be gone as soon as the snow broke up. But the words just wouldn't come.

Spring came as a big relief. The ice broke up quickly and Wilson began trapping again. Once again Nicole occupied her days making willow hoops and stretching skins.

Wilson and Nicole soon left the cabin. They began traveling higher and higher into the Rockies. The days grew warmer and warmer. Finally in May, Wilson said, "Well, you have a choice. I'm going to rendezvous in July."

"Rendezvous?" Nicole asked.

"Every summer trappers meet in one place to sell skins and get supplies. That way we don't have to go back down to St. Louis each summer. This year's rendezvous is at Bear Lake. That's just across the Green River.

"Anyway, I promised I'd take you to the Yellowstone River. I can do that now—before rendezvous. Or you could come to the rendezvous with me. A lot of Indians show up. I imagine the Crow people will be there. You could meet some of your relatives. Then maybe you'd be able to catch a ride back to St. Louis. All the suppliers will be going back overland after rendezvous."

"I don't want to trouble you anymore than I already have," Nicole said as brightly as she could manage. "I'll just go to the rendezvous with you." She felt angry at him for planning to get rid of her. So she added, "And I'll be sure to see that no one takes advantage of me on account of my money."

Wilson just kept riding. He didn't answer.

Nicole couldn't quite believe he'd send her back across the country with strangers. Of course he'd offered to take her back when it was easier. But she had refused. Once again Nicole checked her anger. She was the one in the wrong, not Wilson. She couldn't blame him in the least.

She decided to make the most of the remaining journey. Spring alpine flowers bloomed each day now, as the two travelers drew closer and closer to the peaks. Soon she would meet other Crow Indians. Rendez-vous would be exciting. She tried to be thankful for the opportunity to make this trip at all.

But how she dreaded returning to St. Louis! She supposed she could rent a room there and write her book. But what a lonely life that would be. She couldn't imagine being without the mountains, streams, flowers, and trees. And without Wilson.

Rendezvous at Bear Lake

Nicole shouted for joy when they reached the Continental Divide at South Pass. Wilson laughed with her.

"I made it!" Nicole said breathing hard. "I guess the months of tracking through the brush paid off."

Huge peaks poked into the sky from every direction. From here on, every stream they passed was on its way to the Pacific Ocean rather than the Atlantic.

A few days later, they came down the western side of the pass and crossed the Green River. Nicole and Wilson stood on a hill above Bear Lake. They looked down on the scene below. As if they were at a huge carnival, people crowded about the lake's meadow. Indian and white men raced horses. Dozens of covered wagons operated as makeshift stores. The shouts of men echoed off the mountains. They were having the times of their lives. So this was rendezvous!

"Let's go!" Nicole cried.

Wilson gave her one of his serious looks, and she braced herself for more advice. "Uh, Nicole, the men get pretty wild at rendezvous. You should—"

"I'll manage fine, Wilson, thank you." She was tired of being told how to act with other men. He nodded, and started down the hill behind her.

For another week, more men and a few women continued to arrive. Whole tribes of Indians arrived at once. Caravans of merchants came with goods to sell for sky-high prices. There were hundreds of trappers, a few doctors, several preachers—all kinds of people looking for profit and fun. Many trappers spent every penny they'd earned on horse racing and cards.

When the Crow Indians arrived, they looked for Nicole right away. Word of her presence in the West had raced up the Missouri much faster than she had. At first, she and her Indian cousins just looked at each other shyly. None of them seemed to know what to say or do.

The trappers who spoke both languages fought to be Nicole's interpreter. Through them, she asked endless questions about her mother and father. She laughed and cried as the Crow Indians told her story after story. After so many years, she now knew beyond all doubt that her parents had been wonderful people.

Wilson had been right about the trappers. A group of them followed Nicole wherever she went. Many never saw women except once a year at rendezvous. Then they made the most of it.

Nicole made the most of it, too. Once the men realized she wanted to hear about her parents, they competed to tell the best stories. Sometimes she was sure they made up stories just to get her attention! When she grew tired of the men hovering around, she shooed them away. Sometimes she walked up in the mountains to be alone.

The one person she saw very little of was Wilson. Once in a while, as she sat in the center of a circle of men, she'd see him walk by. He wore that frowning look she'd grown to recognize. But it didn't bother her. Let the sourpuss think what he wanted! She was having the time of her life.

One time Wilson came right up to her and said, "Have you found a ride?"

"Wilson, I'm not going back to St. Louis with strangers."

He looked at his boots. "I suppose I can take you back then."

"Don't be ridiculous. I have already taken advantage of you. I won't trouble you anymore. I have other plans."

"Well, what are you going to do?" he asked.

Nicole wished she could tell him what she really wanted. Instead she said, "I thought I could set up some kind of business near a fort. Sew or cook for the trappers."

Wilson laughed. "You've told me yourself what a poor seamstress you are. And you know little about mountain cooking."

Nicole became angry—and hurt. "Well, in any case, you needn't concern yourself about me," she said. "I shall take care of myself from here on out. You are free to go as you please. I am so sorry I've detained you this long. Thank you for your hospitality."

Wilson walked away. He was sorry he'd hurt Nicole's feelings. He hadn't meant to point out what she *wasn't* good at. She was very good at many useful things. He'd only meant to convince her that she needed him. But he'd done the opposite. And now she had quite clearly dismissed him. Of course, he knew there were many trappers far more attractive than he was. He wouldn't be surprised if she married before rendezvous ended.

On her tenth day at Bear Lake, Nicole watched a man limp down the hill toward the lake. A lot of rough-looking characters came to rendezvous. But however they *looked*, most were hardier than the pine trees growing around the lake. However, this one coming down the hill looked a breath away from being dead.

Nicole kept watching the man. Soon he stumbled and fell. He rolled several yards before he could stop himself. Even then he couldn't get to his feet.

"Dr. Smith!" she called to a doctor who was placing bets on that day's races.

"Just a minute, sweetheart," he called back.

"A man collapsed on the hill," she yelled.

Dr. Smith and a few other men ran up the slope. They carried the man to Dr. Smith's wagon. He moaned so loudly that Nicole could hear him from where she sat.

The following day Nicole went to check on Dr. Smith's patient. Looking in the wagon, she saw a man so thin she could almost count each bone. He was covered with bruises and scrapes as well.

The man opened his eyes. To her horror, Nicole recognized him.

"Andrew!" she gasped.

Andrew Roscoe snarled like a rabid dog.

"Is there anything I can do to help?" Nicole asked. She wondered what awful things he'd been through since she had seen him last. She wondered if the rest of the men on the expedition were even alive.

The wilderness seemed to have claimed Andrew Roscoe entirely. When he finally spoke, he called Nicole a name that even the roughest trappers wouldn't have spoken in her presence.

Nicole sadly left the doctor's wagon. How strange, she thought, that the wilderness had given her life while it seemed to have taken Andrew's away! Starvation and hardship had made him quite mad. She knew she had Wilson's skill to thank for her survival. That thought made her even sadder.

The month passed too quickly. Before Nicole knew it, trappers began packing up and riding away. Some of the supply wagons started rolling eastward. One of them carried the pitiful Andrew Roscoe.

Then the Crow Indians said goodbye and left for their home on the Yellowstone River. At their departure, Nicole panicked. She knew she couldn't really start a business at a fort. If she was going to catch a ride back East, she had better make arrangements fast.

Of course, she'd had dozens of offers of marriage. But none of them interested her. How could men who didn't even know her want to marry her?

Nicole knew what she wanted. But it seemed to be the only thing that wasn't offered. So she decided to take matters into her own hands. Gathering all her courage, she marched to Wilson's tepee.

"When are you leaving?" she asked.

"Soon, I suppose," he said sadly. "I'm worried about you, though. I don't like the idea of your setting up a business out here alone."

"Yes, I know. It was a foolish idea."

"Not foolish, but, well, you need to be a bit more prepared."

"Of course," she agreed.

"So you'll be going back to St. Louis?" he asked.

"I'd rather not."

"What would you rather do?"

Nicole took a deep breath. If she could climb the Continental Divide, she could say the next sentence. "I'd rather marry you."

Wilson looked as if someone had punched him. Nicole turned to run out. But he jumped up and caught her wrist.

"Wait," he said. "That's what you really want?"

Tears stung Nicole's eyes. She felt so ridiculous. What kind of woman asked a man to marry her?

Wilson said, "But you could marry any trapper out here. You're . . . you're so beautiful!"

Tears streamed down her face now. And Wilson felt as awkward as a newborn pup.

"Nicole, there's nothing I'd like better," he said. "I, well—I just never dreamed that you cared for me. All you talked about was seeing Yellowstone country. Why, I knew I loved *you* from the moment I saw you."

Wilson blushed so red Nicole had to giggle even though she was crying. He went on, "I have to admit the only reason I didn't offer to take you home earlier was because I didn't want you to go."

Sniffing, Nicole said, "I tried my best to learn everything I could to help you. I wanted to be so good that you wouldn't be able to do without me."

"I wouldn't want to," Wilson said taking her in his arms.

"All winter you were so cranky, though," she said. "I thought you were sick of me."

"No, no. I didn't see how I'd ever spend a winter *without* you. I was cranky because I was trying to harden my heart. I couldn't bear to think about your leaving."

"I'm not going anywhere," Nicole said. "To me, each day of this journey has felt more like my journey home."

Wilson grinned. "Well, I did promise to take you to Yellowstone country. That's my usual trapping territory. I'll be headed there in a few days. Maybe we should get married and you can come along."

The very next day, Nicole and Wilson found the last remaining preacher at Bear Lake. They set up a chapel under a stand of pines. And with the Rocky Mountains towering above, Nicole and Wilson were married.